The Butterfly

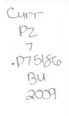

To my great aunt Marcelle Solliliage
and her daughter, my aunt Monique Boisseau Gaw—
two very courageous women I will love
as long as I live.

The Butterfly

PATRICIA POLACCO

PUFFIN BOOKS

It was unusually bright that night outside of Monique's small bedroom window in Choisy-le Roi, just outside of Paris. The moon was so radiant, it seemed almost festive. As Monique gazed up at it, she thought that the moon must not know that her village was occupied by Nazi troops. All of France was, for that matter. There was a terrible war raging in what, to Monique, seemed like most of the world.

But this night the moon seemed not to care. She pulled Pinouff, her cat, up next to her and hugged and kissed her goodnight, then drifted off to sleep.

Monique didn't quite know why she woke up, but suddenly she saw a ghostly little figure sitting just next to the window on the end of her bed. A girl about her own age. She was petting Pinouff.

"Who are you?" Monique whispered.

The ghost child wheeled and looked with sad eyes that seemed frightened, then spun and ran from the bedroom.

The next morning at breakfast, Monique could hardly wait to talk to her mother about the ghost, but her mother seemed almost angry. It wasn't like Marcelle Solliliage to be angry at anyone. "It was only a dream, child . . . do you hear! Only a dream. Now go to school. God knows how much longer you will have the privilege of going to school with the war . . ." Her mother's voice trailed off.

Monique couldn't wait to get to school so that she could tell her best friend, Denise, about the ghost. Since Monique was an only child, Denise was like a sister to her.

On their way home from school that afternoon, Denise asked Monique, "What did this ghost look like?"

"She was dark, and had very sad eyes . . . ," Monique answered.

"Weren't you very, very frightened?" Denise asked.

"At first, yes, but the longer I looked at her, a feeling came over me. A feeling of fear for her," Monique answered.

They stopped and peered into the front window of Monsieur Marks' candy shop. He waved them in as he always did. He loved the children in the neighborhood and always had small bits of brightly wrapped candies for them in his apron pocket.

As the girls entered the store, they saw that most of the jars that used to be filled with every kind of candy and confection were empty. The war.

But Monsieur Marks had saved something for them! "For you, little Monique," Monsieur Marks cooed as he dropped a bright dot of sweetness into her hand. "And one for you, *ma petite*," he said as the beautifully wrapped confection rolled into Denise's waiting hands.

Monique and Denise unwrapped their candies and popped them into their mouths. But as they were walking away from the store, they suddenly saw tall boots coming toward them up the hill.

The tall shining boots of marching Nazi soldiers. Their heels clicked like gunshots along the cobblestone path. People froze and tried not to look at the soldiers. The girls wanted to run, but knew better. They had learned to chat and laugh as if they had no cares in the world.

"Are they looking at us?" Monique asked breathlessly when they had gotten a distance away.

Denise looked back. "No, they're still marching."

Then they heard loud yelling and glass breaking. They both wheeled and looked. To their horror they saw Monsieur Marks being dragged from his shop by the Nazi soldiers.

"*Schwein . . . Judenschwein!*" they heard the Nazis shout as they pushed Monsieur Marks to the ground. They watched the Nazis kick him hard in the ribs with those tall black boots. Monique covered her mouth to hold back a scream. Then a car drove up, and the Nazis threw Monsieur Marks into the back of it.

"Don't look for too long, Monique!" Denise warned. "If we do, they'll come for us next."

The girls were both sobbing by the time they ran up Rue du Bonnard to Monique's mother's house. They knew it had happened before during these years of the occupation, but never had they seen it. And to Monsieur Marks!

"Why . . . why, *Maman*, did they do that to Monsieur Marks?" Monique choked through sobs.

"The Nazis hate people like Monsieur Marks, *ma chérie*. It is so pointless and cruel. . . ." Her voice faded to a whisper.

"What do you mean, people like Monsieur Marks, Maman?" Monique asked again.

"You know, Monique," her mother answered. "Jews."

"But Monsieur Marks is a Frenchman!" Denise said.

Marcelle hugged them both. "The Nazis can't be here forever, my sweet children. Mother France has been here for centuries. They, for a short, terrible time." Marcelle had tears in her eyes.

"Now I'll fix you some soothing tea. Monsieur Marks would not want either of you to worry or be sad."

"Madame!" a voice called from the front door. It was Père Voulliard, their priest from St. Germain des Prés. He rushed in. "Have you heard what happened to Monsieur Marks?"

Marcelle motioned to him to come into the other room, and they closed the door. Monique was used to her mother having hushed conversations in the living room, especially since the war.

Many nights passed and Monique didn't see the little ghost again. But late one night Monique awoke with a start to see her little ghost sitting on the window seat. This time it was holding Pinouff. Monique thought, This is no dream, I can hear Pinouff purring.

"I see you there," Monique whispered.

The little ghost sprang to her feet, but Monique stopped her from running away this time.

"Don't be afraid, it's all right for you to be here!"

The little ghost with sad eyes sat down and said nothing.

"What is your name? Where do you come from?" Monique asked.

The girl just sat for the longest time, holding on tightly to Pinouff. "I once had a cat just like this one," she finally said.

"Her name is Pinouff. What is yours?" Monique sat down by her.

"My name is Sevrine . . . Sevrine."

"Where do you live?" Monique whispered.

"I have lived in many places since the war," the ghostly Sevrine answered.

"Where do you live now? Your parents must miss you, especially in the middle of the night like this."

The girl didn't answer.

"Where do you live?" Monique insisted.

"Here!" Sevrine finally said.

"Here?" Monique said with such surprise and so loudly that it might have awakened the whole neighborhood! "But I live here!"

Sevrine motioned Monique to follow her. They both tiptoed down the stairs and crept into the day room. There Monique saw the rug pulled back and what looked like a door in the floor.

Sevrine pulled up the door, and they both climbed down a very narrow set of stairs into a part of the cellar that Monique didn't even know existed. The walls were scraped clean, and there was a small table with a tiny tray and supper dishes on it. Monique could see another small room with cots. It looked like people were sleeping on them.

"My mother and father and I have been here for a very long time," Sevrine whispered. "We are being hunted by the Nazis, you know. We are Jews. There are many of us hiding all over France."

"But how have you stayed here without my maman knowing?"

"Oh . . . Madame Solliliage? She knows! We aren't the only ones that she has helped."

How could this have been happening in her own home, and her mother never said a word to her about it?

"Your mother made me promise that I would never come to your room again while you were there!"

"I don't understand!"

"It puts you in great danger to know about me. She is protecting you!"

Monique started to say more, but it sounded like footsteps echoing upstairs. Could Marcelle have heard them?

"*Vite*, vite, Monique!" Sevrine pushed her up out of the hidden room.

"But when will I see you again?" Monique whispered as the door closed over the top of her new friend.

The next morning at breakfast Monique didn't know what to say to her mother. Somehow she seemed mysterious. But she chatted to Monique cheerfully, as always. "Go to your garden, my sweet child, and cut some of your beautiful flowers for our table, won't you?"

Monique skipped out of the kitchen doors into her garden with Pinouff trotting after her.

Pinouff was playing with the petals of the flowers as Monique cut them and put them into the basket, when all at once the cat crouched and made herself flat against the ground. Her eyes were ablaze! Then Monique saw why. *A papillon*, a butterfly, fluttered from flower to flower. As it landed on a bright blue iris near the wall, Monique gathered Pinouff into her lap.

"No, ma petite, just look. See how beautiful?" They both sat quietly as they watched the butterfly together.

Suddenly the air grew still and heavy. The birds in the garden stopped singing. Pinouff hid herself in the folds of Monique's apron. Monique looked over the wall and saw tall shiny boots. Her heart leapt in her chest. Three Nazi soldiers glared at her. One reached over the wall and took the butterfly in his leather-covered fist. *"Joli, n'est-ce pas?"* He grinned at Monique, then squeezed his fist. The other tall boots laughed. They mumbled something and walked away.

"Maman, Maman! Tall boots!" Monique shrieked as she ran into the house and blurted out what had happened in the garden.

"*Sacre bleu!* Those monsters!" her mother grumbled as she held her child as close as she could.

"Maman," Monique finally sobbed, "did they do to Monsieur Marks what they did to the butterfly?" Her mother did not answer. She rocked Monique gently and stared out of the window.

But Monique had her answer. Now she understood the sadness in Sevrine's eyes. The fear that was in the eyes of her neighbors and friends whenever the Nazi soldiers came close. She knew now she had to protect her friend. At all costs she had to keep the secret that lived in her basement.

From that time on, Sevrine came to Monique's room as often as she could without waking her own parents or Monique's mother. Marcelle could never know! When the girls were together, they played dress up and had midnight tea parties. They laughed and giggled, and told each other their dreams.

Monique collected things from the outside world for Sevrine to see and feel and touch.

"What did you bring me tonight?" Sevrine asked softly one night.

Monique reached into a small cloth bag and sprinkled rich black earth into Sevrine's hands. "This smells like the air outside," Monique told her. Then she handed Sevrine a bright flower from her garden. "This will be your sunshine. And now, close your eyes!" Monique slowly opened her cupped hands. "Look." It was a glorious butterfly.

"A papillon!" Sevrine whispered in wonder.

Monique put the butterfly near Sevrine's cheek.

"Let its wings flutter," Monique whispered.

Sevrine caught her breath and smiled.

"Like the kiss of an angel!" Monique said softly.

Tears began to fill Sevrine's eyes and roll down her cheeks. "I miss my home, Monique. My own bed. My own kitty, my garden."

"The Nazis won't be here forever. Maman says that they will lose this war," Monique reassured her.

"At our home," Sevrine went on, "we celebrated Shabbat, the holidays . . . Passover, Hanukkah. . . . My mother cooked for days. Family came from everywhere. Then it all changed. We had to leave. My parents were afraid that the Nazis would kill us."

"You'll be home someday, you'll see!"

"Papa is so sick from breathing damp air. He hasn't seen sunlight for months. Maman has to cover his mouth with a pillow so that his coughing can't be heard upstairs."

"I promise, Sevrine, someday you'll be as free as . . . as that papillon."

"Let it fly now, Monique," Sevrine said. "When it flies, it will be as if Papa, Maman, and I are flying away!"

The girls took the butterfly to the open bedroom window and threw it into the night air, then stood and watched it until they couldn't see it anymore.

All of a sudden they looked up—for what reason, who knew. They saw Monsieur Lendormy, the man next door, looking right at them from his window across the courtyard.

Monique's heart leapt in her chest. Sevrine slid down under the windowsill so that Monsieur Lendormy couldn't see her. The girls looked at each other in sheer terror. They knew they had to tell Marcelle.

They ran to her room and awoke her. She was startled to see the two of them together! When they told her about their secret meetings and Monsieur Lendormy, Marcelle sank to her knees in front of them. *"Mon dieu,* mon dieu," she said mournfully as she rocked with fear.

"Are you angry, Madame Solliliage?" Sevrine asked as she began to cry.

"Oh, no, ma petite. No, of course I am not angry. You are a little girl. You didn't ask for this war, or to be kept in my cellar. You needed to play— children need other children." Marcelle smoothed her hair. "But you are no longer safe here, my dear.

"We must leave home tonight." Marcelle began to pull on her clothes. "We need to get you and your family out of the country. Let me see. Père Voulliard will take your parents to the next refuge. You will travel with Monique and me! Yes! Hurry, petites, put on as many clothes as you can. Dress in layers. We can't carry valises, or we will attract attention."

The girls watched as Marcelle, Père Voulliard, and Sevrine's parents dug holes in the cellar floor and buried everything that would look like someone had lived there. Then it was time for them all to leave. Her parents came out dressed as a nun and priest. They both cried as they held Sevrine and said their goodbyes. They would next meet in a village in southern France near the Swiss border.

"God be with us this night!" Père Voulliard prayed.

"*Adonai Yihieh Etanu Halailah*," Sevrine's father prayed as he cried. "God will be with us tonight."

It seemed that Monique, Sevrine, and Marcelle had walked for miles in darkness. Through back alleys, avoiding street lamps. Taking great care to be as quiet as it was possible to be.

With the first light of dawn they had reached the countryside. They stopped to rest under a grove of trees, close to their rendezvous with the people who would take Sevrine to her parents.

Marcelle had just given the girls some bread and cheese, when she pulled them both into a ditch. She motioned for them to be still and quiet. A patrol car full of Nazi soldiers slowly drove by on the country road.

After the car passed, the three sat without speaking.

Finally, another car came driving slowly down the road. It stopped by the bridge a few hundred feet away, and turned its headlights on and off three times.

"It's time, my precious child," Marcelle whispered as she pushed Sevrine out of the ditch, and they ran toward the car. "These people will help you and your maman and papa."

At the car, Monique took something from the pouch she'd been carrying. It was Pinouff! "Take her, Sevrine," Monique whispered.

Tears welled up in Sevrine's eyes. She folded Pinouff into her sweater, then reached into her pocket and pulled out a fine gold chain on which hung a gold Star of David. "Remember me, Monique!"

"We are practically home, my little one," Marcelle said as she and Monique arrived at the train station in Melun. This was where they would board the train to go back to Choisy-le Roi.

But there was an unusual amount of travelers for that early time of day. The station was crowded. Nazi soldiers were everywhere, stopping people, searching them, and barking orders. Marcelle took her daughter's hand. In the other, Monique clutched the chain.

As Monique and Marcelle drew closer and closer to the gate where their papers would be checked, Marcelle pulled a bundle of tickets and documents from her handbag. The entire station of people had to squeeze through the tiny gate to board the train.

Suddenly, the crowd behind Monique and her mother surged and pushed so hard, Monique lost Marcelle's hand. Monique couldn't see her mother anymore. People pushed and shoved, and Monique lost her footing and fell. When she did, Sevrine's necklace slid out of her hand onto the platform floor.

Quickly, she put it into her pocket, pulled herself to her feet, slipped into the line that was pushing through the checkpoint, and was swept with them into a shabby coach car.

The tall boots were shouting at everyone. What if they searched her and found the necklace? And where was her maman?

She could see through the window of her train car people standing on the platform waiting to catch a train going in the opposite direction. Had her mother been pushed into that line instead of onto this train? She tried to see through her own tears to find her mother's face, when she saw a girl alone. She looked thin and sad, very sad. Like Sevrine!

On the girl's coat was a yellow Star of David. Was it Sevrine? No, she could see now, it wasn't Sevrine.

But it could have been.

Monique held Sevrine's necklace tight in her pocket.

"Oh, Maman, Maman, where are you?" she cried as the train lurched away.

The train rolled to a noisy stop. *St. Georges*, the sign read. Only two kilometers from Choisy-le Roi! From home. Monique walked through alleys and back streets that only hours before she, Sevrine, and Maman had passed. "Oh, Maman!" she cried as she walked.

When Monique finally saw the familiar threshold of her front door, she pushed it open and climbed the stairs. She could still smell her mother's scent in the air. She was tired, so tired. She threw herself across her bed and fell into a deep sleep.

Then she dreamed of her mother's voice. "Ma chérie . . . ma petite," the voice said. She dreamt a cool hand crossed her brow. It seemed so real.

When she opened her eyes, she saw that the hand was real! The voice was real!

It was her maman!

"Oh, my sweet brave little girl!" her mother cried as they rocked in each other's arms. "I just knew that I would find you here."

One week passed, two. Monique tried to imagine that Sevrine and her maman and papa, and of course, Pinouff, were safe. Then the tall boots would march by her front gate, reminding her how hopeless it seemed. If only she had a message from Sevrine. A sign. Something.

And then one day, Monique and Marcelle were planting next year's bulbs in the garden, when Marcelle suddenly gasped.

"*Regarde*, Monique, look!" Her mother pointed at the bleak sky above them. A butterfly fluttered down into the garden. And another. *And another.*

They both watched as butterflies started to land on the dry stalks of faded flowers. First there were three, then ten, then twenty and thirty.

Neighbors came out of their cottages and peered over the wall in wonder.

"It's a sign, Maman, a miracle! Sevrine sent them, I know it! She and her parents are safe!"

Monique held up her hand, and a butterfly fluttered and landed on her finger. She took it to her cheek. Its wings fluttered. "A kiss," Monique said softly.

Author's Note

Marcelle Solliliage was part of the French underground and resistance organized by General Charles de Gaulle. Marcelle and many other selfless citizens of France made their own homes a safe haven for Jews escaping to freedom during the terrible Nazi occupation. They did this at great peril to their own lives as well as the lives of their families.

According to my aunt Monique, her mother, Marcelle, was part of the underground and resistance from the very beginning of the Nazi occupation of France. Monique was totally unaware until she met Sevrine, but even then was not aware of the extent of her mother's involvement until the end of the war.

Within two years of the liberation of France, Monique and Marcelle received a letter. In it was a card with a drawing of a papillon inscribed on the cover. Inside it said: "*Je vis!* (I live!) Sevrine." Next to her signature was a paw print.

It was learned later that neither parent survived their attempt to escape. Sevrine was delivered to Switzerland and eventually made it to England, where she remained with close friends of the family for the duration of the war. Some time later she relocated in the new state of Israel with relatives. Monique and Sevrine are friends to this day.

Thirty years after the end of the war, Marcelle contacted local Jewish agencies and asked them to unearth possessions that were buried in her basement by families that never returned to reclaim them.

PATRICIA LEE GAUCH, EDITOR

PUFFIN BOOKS
Published by the Penguin Group
Penguin Young Readers Group, 345 Hudson Street, New York, New York 10014, U.S.A.
Penguin Group (Canada), 90 Eglinton Avenue East, Suite 700,
Toronto, Ontario, Canada M4P 2Y3 (a division of Pearson Penguin Canada Inc.)
Penguin Books Ltd, 80 Strand, London WC2R 0RL, England
Penguin Ireland, 25 St Stephen's Green, Dublin 2, Ireland
(a division of Penguin Books Ltd)
Penguin Group (Australia), 250 Camberwell Road, Camberwell, Victoria 3124, Australia
(a division of Pearson Australia Group Pty Ltd)
Penguin Books India Pvt Ltd, 11 Community Centre, Panchsheel Park, New Delhi - 110 017, India
Penguin Group (NZ), 67 Apollo Drive, Rosedale, North Shore 0632, New Zealand
(a division of Pearson New Zealand Ltd)
Penguin Books (South Africa) (Pty) Ltd, 24 Sturdee Avenue, Rosebank, Johannesburg 2196, South Africa

Registered Offices: Penguin Books Ltd, 80 Strand, London WC2R 0RL, England

First published in the United States of America by Philomel Books,
a division of Penguin Putnam Books for Young Readers, 2000
Published by Puffin Books, a division of Penguin Young Readers Group, 2009

7 9 10 8

THE LIBRARY OF CONGRESS HAS CATALOGED THE PHILOMEL BOOKS EDITION AS FOLLOWS:
Polacco, Patricia.
The butterfly / written and illustrated by Patricia Polacco.
p. cm.
Summary: During the Nazi occupation of France, Monique's mother hides a Jewish family
in her basement and tries to help them escape to freedom.
ISBN: 0-399-23170-6 (hc)
1. Jews—France Juvenile fiction. 2. World War, 1939–1945—France Juvenile fiction. 3. France—History—German occupation,
1940–1945 Juvenile fiction. [1. Jews—France Fiction. 2. World War, 1939–1945—France Fiction.
3. France—History—German occupation, 1940–1945 Fiction.] I. Title.
PZ7.P75186 Pap 2000 [Fic]—dc21 99-30038 CIP

Puffin Books ISBN 978-0-14-241306-7

Manufactured in the United States of America

Book design by Semadar Megged.
The text is set in 16-point Adobe Jenson Semibold.